Playtime Friends
STORY
TREASURY

This book belongs to

....

....

EGMONT

We bring stories to life

This edition published in 2008 by Dean,
an imprint of Egmont UK Limited
239 Kensington High Street
London W8 6SA

Edited by Brenda Apsley and designed by Jeannette O'Toole

ISBN 978 0 6035 6289 1
3 5 7 9 10 8 6 4 2
Printed in Italy

Playtime Friends
STORY
TREASURY

DEAN

Playtime Friends STORY TREASURY

**A special collection of
Thomas the Tank Engine, Bob the Builder,
Postman Pat® and Fireman Sam stories**

Contents

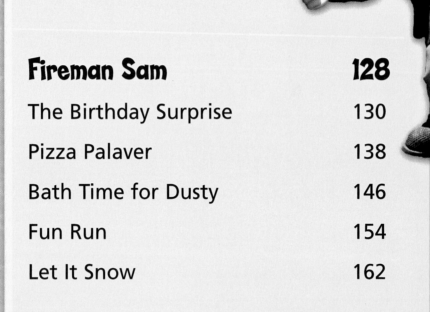

Postman Pat

Greendale is a friendly village.

Pat Clifton is the village postman. Everyone calls him Postman Pat.

Jess, Pat's cat, goes everywhere with him.

Sara Clifton, Pat's wife, works at the railway station.

Julian is Pat and Sara's son.

Mrs Goggins looks after the Post Office. **Bonnie** is her dog.

Reverend Timms is the village vicar.

Ted Glen, the handyman, can mend all sorts of things.

PC Selby is a policeman. His daughter, **Lucy**, is seven.

Julia Pottage keeps cows and sheep on her farm. She has twins called **Katy** and **Tom**.

Ajay Bains runs the railway. His wife **Nisha** works in the station café.

Dorothy and **Alf Thompson** have a farm. **Bill** is their son.

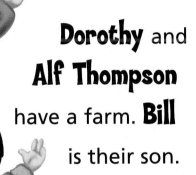

They have a daughter called **Meera** and a baby called **Nikhil**.

Doctor Gilbertson is the doctor. Her daughter, **Sarah**, is eight.

Jeff Pringle is the school teacher. His son is **Charlie**.

I made a film about Greendale with my new video camera. But when I showed it, I got some real surprises! Find out what happened in . . .

The Greendale Movie

Postman Pat had a new video camera. He said, "Smile please, Mrs Goggins!"

"Don't film me!" said Mrs Goggins. "Make a film about Greendale instead."

"That's a great idea," said Pat. "I'll show it at the school tonight. Will you tell everyone?"

"Of course I will," said Mrs Goggins.

Pat wasn't sure how to use the camera. "How do I switch it on?" he said. He pressed lots of buttons.

"Meow!" said Jess. He seemed to know!

Pat went to the church. He filmed Reverend Timms playing the piano. When he went out to his van to get the post, the camera was still going . . .

Reverend Timms played rock and roll music. Pat didn't see him!

Pat went to the railway station. Ajay and Ted were cleaning the Greendale Rocket.

Ted grabbed the camera. He wanted to try it.

"Careful!" said Pat. Too late! He dropped the post and it blew away. Pat ran along the platform to catch it.

When Pat got back, Ajay had a bucket of soapy water on his head!

Pat laughed. "That's funny," he said. "Shall I film you?"

"No!" said Ajay. "Not just now!"

That night, Pat showed his film.

Reverend Timms came on the screen. He was playing rock and roll. "I didn't film that!" said Pat.

Then Jess' face filled the screen. "I didn't film that!" said Pat. Next, the film showed Ajay spilling the bucket of water. "I didn't film that!" said Pat.

"Sorry," said Pat. "The camera must have kept going when I wasn't there."

Ted said, "Don't be sorry, Pat. Your film is a good laugh!"

"So you like it?" asked Pat.

"We **love** it, Dad!" said Julian. "It's great!"

"Meow!" said Jess. He agreed with Julian!

It was a tricky time for Ted when sand ended up all over the village green! But it turned into a fun day when Julian and his friends arrived. Find out what happened in . . .

At the Seaside

It was the school holidays. Pat had a postcard for Meera.

"It's from cousin Sanjay!" she said. "He's on holiday at the seaside. Can we go, Mum? Can we, Dad?"

"It's too far," said Ajay. "We'll have a picnic in Greendale instead. Come on!"

Ted was driving past the village green with a load of sand.
His lorry went over a bump and the flap came undone. Sand
poured out on to the grass!

PC Selby arrived. "That sand can't stay there, Ted," he said.
He scooped up some sand in his helmet.

"This is going to take all day," said Ted.

"You need something to put the sand into," said Pat.

"Meow!" said Jess. He knew just the thing! He pulled some mailbags out of Pat's van.

Pat and Ted put sand into the mailbags. But it ran through the gaps!

Pat put the sand in a wheelbarrow. But when he pushed it up a plank on to Ted's lorry it fell off!

Pat used a vacuum cleaner to suck up the sand. The bag got bigger and bigger – but then it burst! Pat and the others were covered in sand!

The Bains family walked to Thompson Ground. They put their picnic on the grass.

"BUZZZZZ! BUZZZZZ!" went Dorothy's bees!

"Get away from my sandwich!" said Ajay. "Come on.

We'll have our picnic at Greendale Farm instead."

But the field at Greendale Farm was full of sheep!

"Baaaa!" they said. They wanted to eat the picnic!

"Oh, let's just go home," said Meera.

Julian and his friends played in the sand on the village green with their buckets and spades. "It's just like a beach!" said Julian. Meera smiled when she saw the village green beach. She got her day out at the seaside, after all!

One day, Julian had some news. There was going to be a pet show on the village green. He was going to enter Jess. But Sarah had other ideas! Read all about it in . . .

The Pet Show

Julian told Sarah Gilbertson there was going to be a pet show. "Are you going to enter?" he asked.

"No," said Sarah. "I haven't got a pet."

Just then, Jess appeared. "Here's Jess," said Julian.

"Great! I can take Jess to the show!" Sarah said.

Julian didn't know what to say! "Er . . . I didn't mean that . . ."

Sarah went off with Jess. "Thanks, Julian!" she said.

"MEOW!" said Jess.

"I need to make you pretty for the show, Jess," said Sarah.

But Jess doesn't like being combed. He ran away!

At the school, Mr Pringle and Charlie were chasing Dotty the guinea pig.

"**Squeak!**" said Dotty.

"**MEOW!**" said Jess.

Dotty ran into her cage.

"Thanks, Jess," said Charlie.

"**Je-ess!**" called Sarah.

"Where are you?"

"**MEOW!**" said Jess.

Jess ran to Greendale Farm.
Tom and Katy were chasing
their sheep, Parsley and Sage.
"Baaaaa!" said the sheep.
"MEOW!" said Jess.
The sheep ran into their pen.
"Thanks, Jess!" said Tom.

Jess met Mrs Goggins' dog, Bonnie.

"We've lost her ball," said Meera.

"Je-ess!" called Sarah.

"Where are you?"

Jess hid behind a barrel until Sarah went away. Then he found Bonnie's ball.

"Thanks, Jess!" said Meera.

Jess went to the pet show.

"There's a special prize for . . . Jess!"
said Reverend Timms. "It's for being helpful.
He helped catch Dotty . . ."

"And Parsley and Sage," said Tom.

"And he found Bonnie's ball," said Meera.

"MEOW!" said Jess.

When the circus was cancelled, the children put on their own show. Bill didn't think he was good at anything – until he made me laugh! Read what happened in . . .

Clowning Around

Mr Pringle was taking the children to the circus. But the show was cancelled!

"Can we put on our own circus?" asked Bill.

"Yes!" said Meera. "We can use my uncle's big tent."

Mr Pringle said, "All right then."

Pat went to the railway station to get the tent.

"We'll put it in my van, Ajay," said Pat. "You take one end. I'll take the other."

But the tent was too big!

"We'll carry it to the village green," said Pat.

"Right," said Ajay.

There were lots of helpers on the green. They all knew where the tent should go.

"This way. No, that way."

"Right a bit. Left a bit."

"Turn it round. No, the other way."

At last, the tent was in the right place.

The children got their circus acts ready.

Bill juggled with bean bags. But they landed on his head! **"Ouch!"**

Julian set out flowerpots for Jess to jump on. But Jess jumped on Bill! **"Ouch!"**

Pat smiled. "You make me laugh, Bill!" he said.

"Do I?" said Bill. "I'll be a clown, then. Will you be my partner, Pat?"

On the day of the circus, the children did their acts.

Then Jess did his. It was perfect!

Everyone clapped and cheered.

"Meow!" said Jess.

The clowns were last. Bill squirted water at Pat. Then Pat slipped on a banana skin and landed – **oof!** – on his bottom!

Bill and Pat made everyone laugh.

They were the stars of the show.

"Hurray!" cried the audience. "More! More!"

Bill and Pat took a bow.

"Well done, Bill!" said Pat.

"Thanks, partner!" said Bill.

One winter's day, I took Mrs Goggins for a ride in a hot-air balloon. Ted was the pilot, but we ended up flying off without him! Read about our adventure in . . .

The Big Balloon Ride

Greendale was covered in snow when Pat went to the Post Office one cold winter morning.

Mrs Goggins showed him a magazine about hot-air balloon rides. "What fun!" she said.

Pat drove to the watermill. Ted was shovelling snow. Some hit Pat – **SPLAT!** – and gave him a snowy beard!

"Get your hot-air balloon, Ted," said Pat. "We're taking Mrs Goggins for a ride!"

Ted filled the balloon with air. But – **HISSS!** – it had a leak.

"I'll fix it," said Ted. "You get Mrs Goggins."

PC Selby arrived. "Have you seen a little white dog?" he asked. "I've got to take it to the Dogs' Home. Will you help me find it?"

"All right, Arthur," said Ted. "Here, doggie!"

When Pat got back with Mrs Goggins, Ted had gone.

Mrs Goggins and Pat climbed into the basket. Mrs Goggins turned around and the air control moved from **OFF** to **ON**!

Jess jumped in, too. He undid the rope that kept the balloon on the ground!

The balloon filled with air and floated off! "Oh, no!" said Pat. "We're flying!"

Mr Pringle and the children were on a nature trail. The first thing they found was a little white dog!

Charlie looked for birds. "There's one!" he said. "It's round and red with yellow stripes. It's a . . ."

"Hot-air balloon!" said Julian.

Ted and PC Selby arrived. "That's the little dog I'm looking for!" said PC Selby.

"And that's my balloon!" said Ted. "Let some more air out, Pat. We'll grab the rope!"

The balloon floated down and Pat and Mrs Goggins climbed out.

PC Selby told them about the little dog. "She's got no home," he said.

"That's a shame," said Mrs Goggins. "Can I keep her?"

PC Selby nodded. "Of course you can."

"What are you going to call her?" asked Julian.

"I've had a bonny day," said Mrs Goggins. "I'll call her Bonnie!"

I have to deliver the post no matter how bad the weather is. Read about what happened when my van broke down in . . .

The Tricky Transport Day

It was snowing in Greendale. "Can we make a snowman, Dad?" asked Julian.

"You start it," said Pat. "I'll help after work."

Pat set off. But his van made a funny noise.

He drove to Ted's house. "Can you mend it?" asked Pat.

"Yes," said Ted. "But I'll need all day. Take my truck."

Pat and Jess set off in Ted's truck. But that started making funny noises as well!

"Take my tractor instead," said Alf, when Pat arrived at Thompson Ground.

Pat and Jess took the post to Greendale Station. But when Pat got back on Alf's tractor, it wouldn't go!

Then Ajay arrived on the Greendale Rocket. "Got
a problem, Pat?" he called.

"My van's broken," said Pat. "I'm using Alf's tractor, but
it won't start."

"Use my motorbike," said Ajay.

"Great!" said Pat. "But what about Jess?"

"He can ride in the sidecar!" said Ajay.

Pat and Jess rode along but – **HISS!** – the tyre went flat.

Ajay came along on the Rocket. He gave Pat and Jess a lift to a little station. But they were still a long way from Greendale Farm.

"We'll just have to walk," said Pat.

They met Meera, Bill and Charlie.

"I've got to get the post to Greendale Farm," said Pat.

"Take my sledge," said Bill.

"Er, thanks, Bill," said Pat.

Pat and Jess set off. But the sledge went **VERY** fast.

At the farm, it crashed into some bales of hay. Jess flew into the air and landed in Julia's laundry basket!

Pat had one letter left. It was for Ted.

"Skate there on my roller blades," said Tom.

Pat skated to Ted's house with Jess on his shoulder.

When they got back home, Jess watched Julian make his snowman.

A lump of snow fell on to Jess. "Jess is a **SNOWCAT**!" said Julian.

Thomas the Tank Engine

Lots of engines work on the Railway on the Island of **Sodor**. They are Really Useful!

Thomas is the Number 1 tank engine. Annie and Clarabel are his coaches.

James is the red Number 5 engine.

Edward is the old blue Number 2 engine.

Sir Topham Hatt is in charge of the Railway. The engines call him The Fat Controller.

Henry is the Number 3 engine. He's fast and strong.

Percy, Number 6, always works hard.

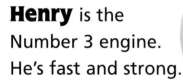

Gordon, Number 4, pulls the Express.

Toby is the Number 7 tram engine.

Harvey, Number 27, is a crane engine.

Harold the helicopter flies all over the Island.

Bill and **Ben** are yellow twin engines.

Cranky the crane loads and unloads things.

Salty shunts trains behind the engines.

Some engines work on the **Narrow Gauge Railway**.

Mr Percival looks after the Narrow Gauge engines. They call him The Thin Controller.

Skarloey is the cheerful Number 1 engine.

Rheneas, Number 2, works with Skarloey.

Rusty is the orange Number 5 diesel.

Duncan, Number 6, doesn't like being told what to do!

Trucks can be very naughty! When The Fat Controller gave me new ones, I wanted to keep them clean. But they had other ideas! Read about them in . . .

Thomas' New Trucks

Thomas was shunting his trucks. It was hard work. He **huffed** and **puffed**. He **biffed** and **bashed** them.

James arrived. "Look!" he said. "The Fat Controller gave me new trucks. They're nicer than yours, Thomas!"

James was right. "My trucks are old," said Thomas. "I want new ones, too!"

Next day, The Fat Controller had a surprise for Thomas. New trucks!

James showed his new trucks to Bill and Ben.

"Peep!" said Thomas. "I've got new trucks too! Look!"

"Yours are shinier than James'!" puffed Ben.

James was cross. "They are shiny now, Thomas," he huffed. "But you won't keep them like that!"

Thomas took his new trucks to the Quarry. **"Must-keep-my-trucks-clean!"** he puffed.

James was there. "There's no dust on my trucks!" he said.

Thomas backed under a hopper. His new trucks went too far. **Whooosh!** They were covered in dust!

James laughed. "Your trucks aren't shiny now!"

Thomas went to the coaling plant. He backed under a hopper. He went **very** slowly. But the trucks went too far again! **Whooosh!** They were covered in coal dust!

Thomas had an idea. "I'll use my old trucks for messy jobs," he said. "Not my new ones."

Thomas took his old trucks to the Docks. But a coupling broke – **SNAP!** Thomas put on his brakes. The trucks bumped into him. All the coal spilled out!

The Fat Controller was cross. "You must use your new trucks, Thomas!" he said.

The trucks got very dirty. But they sang, and rolled along happily. "They **like** being messy," said Thomas. "They would rather be **USEFUL** than clean!"

James' trucks wanted to join in the fun, too.

James backed up to Cranky to collect some melons.

His trucks stopped very quickly.

Squelch! Squish! Squash!

The melons landed on James!

Thomas laughed. **"Peep!"** he said. "Your trucks would rather be **USEFUL** than clean, James. Just like mine!"

Edward is the kind
old blue Number 2 engine.
Gordon said he was too
old to be Useful, but
Edward proved him wrong!
Find out how he did
it in . . .

Edward, the Very Useful Engine

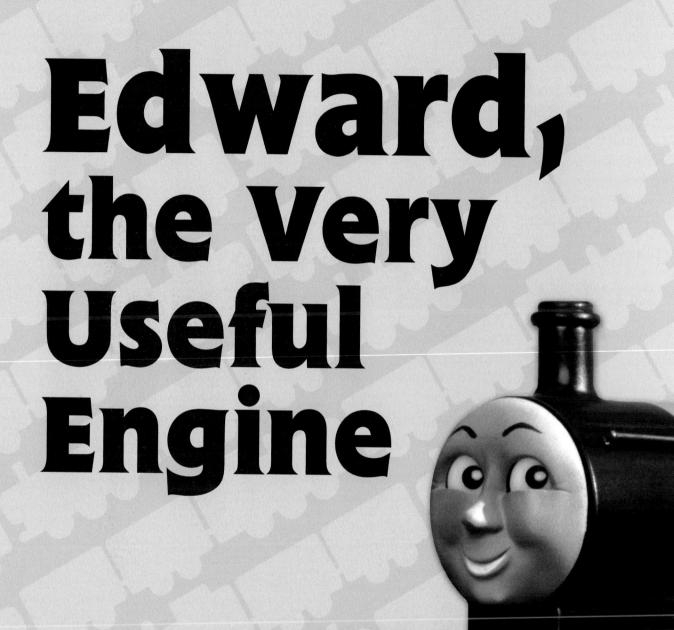

Edward likes working with the trucks. He's a good Back Engine, too. He helps engines when they have heavy loads to pull. He pushes them from the back.

But Gordon said Edward was too old. "He's a useless old steam pot!" he said.

The Fat Controller was cross. "Edward, useless?" he said. "I'll see about that!"

The Fat Controller spoke to Edward. "The new Loop Line is ready," he said. "I want you to teach Stepney how to run it."

"But who will look after the trucks, Sir?" Edward asked.

"Duck will do your work for you," said The Fat Controller.

The big engines heard the news. They were pleased.

"I'm glad Duck is taking Edward's place," said Henry. "Duck is very reliable."

"**Wheesh!**" said Gordon. "Yes. But it doesn't bother me. I never go near the trucks. And I never need a Back Engine."

Edward liked his new job, but Duck didn't like his! It was hard work pulling trucks. Duck went slower . . . and slower . . . and slower. Halfway up a hill, his wheels stopped turning!

"We're stuck," said his Driver. "Gordon will be coming any minute now!" He told the Signalman to put the signals to red.

Gordon stopped at the signals. But when he tried to set off again, his wheels spun.

"We need a Back Engine," said his Driver.

The Fat Controller sent Edward! He pushed Gordon and Duck all the way back to the Station.

"You said rude things about Edward," The Fat Controller told Gordon. "But he is Very Useful."

Gordon agreed. He rolled up to Edward and said, "Thank you for helping me, Edward. You are a Very Useful engine."

"Peep!" said Edward. "I was glad to help!"

We call Harold the Helicopter 'Whirlybird', because he can fly like a bird. One day he was on duty, but he wanted to help with the fête. Find out how he did it in . . .

Harold
and the
Flying
Horse

Summer is a busy time for Harold the helicopter. He flies around making sure the visitors are safe.

The engines were helping with the fête. Percy took the deckchairs and tables.

"Peep!" he whistled to his passengers. "Don't forget the summer fête!"

Harold flew around. He looked down at the engines. They all had jobs to do. He felt a bit jealous. "I want to help with the fête, but I can't," he said. "I have to stay on patrol in case anyone needs help."

Harold flew to the Airfield to get more fuel.

Pegasus the horse was in the next field. He was going to give the children rides in his little painted cart.

"Even Pegasus is helping," said Harold, sadly.

Thomas arrived. "Don't forget the fête, Harold," he said. "Everyone will be there."

"Everyone but me," said Harold. "I'm on duty, so I can't go."

"Oh," said Thomas. "But being a rescue helicopter is a Really Useful job, isn't it?"

Harold knew Thomas was right. But he still wanted to help.

The Fat Controller arrived. "Pegasus is stuck in a ditch!" he told Harold. "We need him at the fête. Can you help him?"

"I'm on my way, Sir!" said Harold.

Percy watched Harold fly away. "Pegasus is a funny name," he said.

"Pegasus was a horse in an old story," said The Fat Controller. "A flying horse."

"A flying horse!" said Percy. **"Wheesh!"**

Thomas was at the ditch when Harold got there. "Can you get Pegasus out?" he asked.

"Yes," said Harold. "I'll put him in my sling and lift him out. Watch!"

The men put the sling around Pegasus. Harold lifted him into the air and took him to the fête.

Percy saw Pegasus up in the air. "Flatten my funnel!" he said. "He really is a flying horse!"

That afternoon, Pegasus took the children for rides in his cart. They said, "Thank you, Pegasus! Thank you, Harold!"

Harold smiled. "I helped with the fête, after all!" he said happily.

Cranky the crane works hard. But sometimes he's naughty. Read about when he knocked down a shed and had to listen to Salty's story in . . .

No Sleep for Cranky

Cranky the crane works at the Docks. He works through the day, then through the night. He never gets a good rest. He's always tired. He works and works and works.

He's so high up that he doesn't have any friends. He doesn't have much to smile about. That's why he's always cranky.

Cranky was working hard
when Salty the diesel arrived.
"Ahoy there, Cranky!" he said.
"You're late!" said Cranky.
"Where have you been?"
"Cranky old Cranky!" said Salty.
Bill and Ben arrived, too. "Hurry
up!" said Cranky. "I haven't got
all day!"

Salty told Cranky a story to cheer him up. It went on . . . and on . . . and on . . .

It made Cranky more cranky than ever! He swung his arm and dropped pipes on to the tracks. They rolled into a shed and knocked it down!

Bill, Ben and Salty were trapped!

"You're going to be in big trouble," said Bill.

Thomas brought The Fat Controller.

"What a mess!" he said. "We can't move the shed until morning. Bill, Ben and Salty will just have to stay here for the night."

That didn't stop Salty talking! When the moon came out he was still telling his story.

Cranky's ears were sore! "If this is what friends are like," he thought, "I don't want any!"

In the morning, Salty's story was still not finished.

Harvey the Crane Engine came to clear up the mess.

"Flatten my funnel!" he said. "Who did this?"

"Cranky!" said Bill.

"I won't do it again," said Cranky. "As long as I don't have to listen to any more of Salty's stories!"

Cranky loaded the trucks carefully and quickly. He even said "please" and "thank you"!

"Peep!" said Thomas. "This isn't like Cranky at all!"

But Thomas spoke too soon! Cranky couldn't help being naughty. He dropped the next load on the rails, right in front of Percy.

He was just as cranky as ever!

I was proud when The
Fat Controller chose me
to bring the circus train.
I wanted to pull it by myself.
But there was trouble! Find
out what happened in . . .

Thomas and the Circus

The engines were very excited. The circus was coming to town!

The Fat Controller asked Thomas to bring the circus train from the Docks.

"If there are too many trucks for you to pull, you must share the work with the other engines," he said.

"Yes, Sir, I will," said Thomas.

At the Docks, the acrobats climbed aboard Annie. Clarabel carried the band.

Salty shunted the heavy train behind Thomas. "Need any help, Matey?" he asked.

"No, thank you, Salty," said Thomas. "I can do it!"

Thomas **huff-huffed** away. His pistons pumped. His traction rods rattled.

Thomas pulled the circus train through Maron Station. It was full of people waving and cheering!

"Peep!" said Thomas. "This is fun!"

Thomas met Percy at the Junction. "Can I take some trucks for you?" asked Percy.

Thomas wanted to pull the train himself. "No, I'll do it on my own," he said.

Thomas puffed on. The train felt heavier. His traction rods rattled. His pistons pumped.

He stopped at a signal. "I'll take some trucks for you," said James. "Let me help you, Thomas."

"No, I can do it on my own," Thomas said.

Then there was trouble! **Creak! Crack!** Thomas'
traction rods broke. He couldn't move!

Driver sent for help and everyone had to get off the train.

James came with the new
traction rods and Percy
brought hay for the horses.
"I wish I'd shared the work
with you two," said Thomas.

Thomas was soon ready to set off again. This time he shared out the trucks. Percy took the horses. James took the clowns. Thomas took the big top tent.

When the circus was ready the engines went to see it.

"Peep!" said Thomas. "Thanks for helping. I didn't know sharing work could be so much **FUN**!"

Duncan doesn't like being told what to do. When Rusty told him not to use the old wooden bridge, he took no notice! Find out who rescued him in . . .

Trusty Rusty

Rusty looks after the Mountain Railway. He and his Driver check the tracks, tunnels and bridges. One day they found cracks in the old wooden bridge.

"Cracks are bad!" said Rusty. "The bridge might fall down."

"We must tell the other engines not to use it!" said his Driver.

Rusty found Skarloey and Duncan. "You must not use the old wooden bridge," he told them. "It's not safe."

Duncan **wheeshed!** "How would you know?" he said, rudely. "Don't tell me what to do!"

Rusty raced down the Mountain Line. He told The Fat Controller about the bridge.

"I'll send men to fix it," said The Fat Controller. "Until they do, no one must use it."

Rusty's Driver put up a sign to say that the bridge was not safe. The engines went up the mountain on a different track.

One day, Duncan needed more coal. But the coal bunker was empty.

"There's another one on the other side of the wooden bridge," said Skarloey. "But Rusty said we can't use it."

"Hah!" puffed Duncan. He steamed on to the bridge. But he forgot that he had no coal! He hissed, and stopped.

Then – **c-r-a-c-k!** – the wood started to split!

Skarloey went to get help. He met Rusty. "Duncan is stuck on the bridge!" he said.

"I'll go and get him," said Rusty.

As Rusty went on to the bridge, the track shook and wobbled. More bits of wood fell off!

"Help!" whistled Duncan.

"I'll save you!" said Rusty.

The Drivers coupled Duncan to Rusty.

C-r-a-c-k! Rusty pulled Duncan off the bridge just before it broke into pieces.

"You should not have used the bridge," The Fat Controller told Duncan. "Rusty told you it wasn't safe."

"Sorry," said Duncan. "Thank you for saving me, Rusty. You were very brave."

"Yes, Rusty, very brave indeed," said The Fat Controller.

Rusty was so proud that he didn't know what to say!

Rheneas and Skarloey
always work together. But
one day Rheneas wanted
to work on his own. Read
about what happened
in . . .

Rheneas
and the
Dinosaur

Rheneas and Skarloey are best friends. They both like shunting trucks. They **biff** and **bash** them all day long. One day, people from the Sodor Museum found some very old bones. They were from a dinosaur!

Mr Percival is The Thin Controller. He looks after the Narrow Gauge railway. "The dinosaur is going to the Museum. I need two very careful engines to take it," he said.

"We're careful!" puffed Rheneas. "Look!"

Rheneas shunted trucks gently. But Skarloey was excited. He forgot about being careful and **crashed** and **bashed** and **bumped** the trucks.

The Thin Controller was cross. "You are not careful engines!" he said.

"I can be careful, Sir! Please let me try," Rheneas said.

"Very well," said Mr Percival.

"I'm sorry I biffed the trucks, Rheneas. Can we try together?" Skarloey said.

"No!" said Rheneas. He steamed away. "I can do it on my own."

Rheneas took coal to the Station Houses. It was hard work pulling the trucks on his own. His pistons pounded and his axles ached. But he kept going.

"You worked very hard today, Rheneas. And you were careful. You can take the dinosaur skeleton. Can you do it on your own?" The Thin Controller said.

"Yes, Sir!" said Rheneas.

But he got a surprise when he saw the dinosaur. It was very, **VERY** big! He had to use all his puff to pull it.

Rheneas chuffed up a steep hill. He went slower and slower. Then he rolled back down again!

Just then, Skarloey arrived!

"Will you help me, please, Skarloey?" asked Rheneas. "The dinosaur is too heavy for me. I was silly to try pulling it on my own. I want us to work together again."

Skarloey buffered up to his friend. They pushed the dinosaur up the hill together.

Then they took it to the Museum.

Thomas brought a man with a camera. He took a photograph of them.

"Smile!" said the man.

Rheneas smiled a big smile. So did Skarloey. They were best friends again.

*I don't like my snowplough!
But when the snow was very
deep, The Fat Controller told
me I'd have to use it.
Find out what
happened
in . . .*

Trouble for Thomas

It was Christmas on Sodor. There were lots of passengers and presents to deliver.

"Driver says there's more snow on the way," said Edward.

"Yes, we'll have to wear our snowploughs," said James.

Thomas doesn't like his snowplough.

"Peep!" he said. "Mine doesn't fit!"

That night it snowed hard. In the morning, the engines had their snowploughs fitted.

The Fat Controller had a job for Thomas. "I want you to bring a Christmas tree," he said. "It's for the village on Toby's Branch Line."

"But my snowplough is too big, Sir," said Thomas. "Can I please have a smaller one?"

"There are no spares," said The Fat Controller. "You'll have to make do, Thomas."

The fitters tried to fit Thomas' snowplough. But it was much too big! It fell off!

"Horrid old thing!" said Thomas. He pulled an angry face. He didn't like that snowplough one little bit!

Later, Thomas steamed to the Docks.

"Make sure you get that tree to Toby safely, young
Thomas!" said Salty.

"I will!" said Thomas.

Thomas took the tree to the station. Toby was there. "I'm
glad you have your snowplough, Thomas," he said. "I can't
clear all this snow by myself."

Thomas and Toby set off. It was hard work, and Thomas' snowplough wasn't working very well. He got stuck! He pushed and pushed – and his snowplough cracked!

It swung to one side like a big knife. It hit the water tower, and knocked it down!

"Cinders and ashes!" said Thomas. "I'll try without my snowplough."

Thomas pushed and pushed. Then he pushed, harder and harder, until . . .

Thomas and Toby steamed into the station!

"Phew!" said Thomas. **"Peep, Peep!"**

Everyone cheered and clapped. "Hooray for Thomas!" they cried. "Hooray for Toby! Hooray for the Christmas tree!"

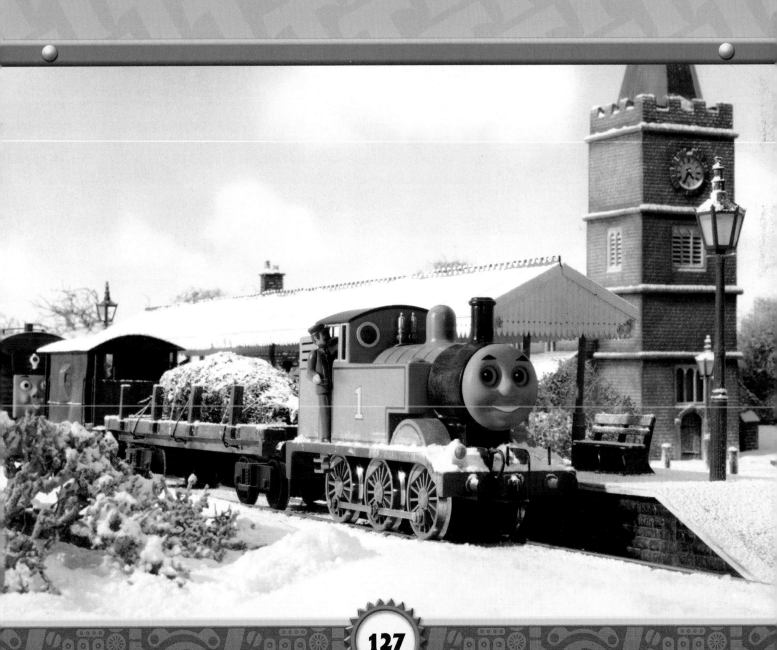

Fireman Sam

Pontypandy is a little town in Wales. The Fire Service has all kinds of emergencies to deal with!

Penny Morris drives **Venus**, the rescue tender.

Fireman Sam drives **Jupiter**, the fire engine.

Elvis Cridlington is the fire station cook.

Twins **Sarah** and **James** are Sam's niece and nephew.

Station Officer Steele is in charge of the fire station.

Dusty the dog doesn't belong to anyone, but everyone looks after him.

Tom Thomas is the pilot of the Mountain Rescue helicopter and drives the jeep.

Mike Flood does odd jobs and helps Tom.

Helen Flood is a nurse.

Mandy is their daughter.

Dilys Price is the owner of the grocery shop.

'Naughty' Norman is her son. **Woolly** is his pet lamb.

Bella Lasagne runs a busy café. **Rosa** is her cat.

Trevor Evans drives the bus.

I didn't get any cards on my birthday this year. I thought everyone had forgotten. But they hadn't! Find out what happened in . . .

The Birthday Surprise

It was Sam's birthday. His friends were planning a surprise party for him in the fire station gym!

Norman's job was to keep Sam away from the station until everything was ready.

Bella was making Sam's birthday cake. Norman brought the candles. "Mam says take extra care with them because . . ." said Norman.

But Norman stopped talking because just then Sam arrived. He was on his way to the fire station!

"I'll, er, come with you," Norman said to Sam.

When they got to the station Elvis wouldn't let them in!

"You've, er, got to say the password!" said Norman.

"That's right," said Elvis. "Security, see."

Sam sighed. "I don't know any password," he said. "I'll have to guess. Is it Bella?"

"No," said Elvis.

"Flea?" said Sam.

"No," said Elvis. "But you're close."

"Dusty?" said Sam.

"Correct!" said Elvis. "Come in, Sam."

Norman had to keep Sam out of the gym.

"Oooo-er . . ." he said, going all wobbly. "I feel funny!"

Sam took Norman home. "Phew!" said Norman.

In the café, Bella and Mandy tested the candles. Bella lit them, then blew them out. Then they went into the kitchen. But the candles lit up again!

Norman and Dusty went to the café. Dusty tried to lick the icing on Sam's cake. It fell off the table and the candles set the curtain on fire!

ACTION STATIONS! Nee Nah! Nee Nah! Sam and Elvis jumped into Jupiter and raced to the café. They soon put the fire out.

At last it was time for the party!

Norman took Sam into the gym.

"SURPRISE!" said everyone. "Happy Birthday, Sam!"

Bella had made Sam a new cake.

Sam blew out the candles. But they lit up again!

"Crikey, Sam," said Norman. "You must be getting short of puff!"

When I helped Mike get Bella's new pizza oven into her café, I didn't think I'd be back there again later! Read about our emergency call-out in . . .

Pizza
Palaver

Sam and Elvis went to Bella's café. There was an oven outside the door.

"Is-a my-a new-a pizza oven," said Bella.

"But it won't go through the door!" said Mike.

Sam knew what to do. He put Bella's rolling pins under the oven. Then he rolled it inside!

Mike fixed it to the chimney.

"Grazie!" said Bella.

Norman and Mandy were playing football. Norman kicked the ball into the air. It hit an old bird's nest on Bella's chimney and fell down inside! "Oops!" said Norman.

"We'd better tell Bella," said Mandy.

When Norman saw the pizza oven, he forgot about the nest. "Can we try making a pizza, Bella?" he asked.

"OK," said Bella. She lit the pizza oven. She didn't know about the bird's nest in the chimney. The flames from the oven set fire to it!

Norman and Mandy made their pizzas.

"Now we-a cook-a them," said Bella.

She put them in the new pizza oven.

A few minutes later, Trevor came in and sniffed. "Those pizzas smell really . . . "

"**Pongy!**" said Norman.

"**Smoky!**" said Mandy.

"**Mamma mia!**" said Bella. "Ai-ai-ai!"

"Everybody out!" said Trevor. "I'm calling the fire station!"

Sam and Elvis raced to the café. Bella and the others were waiting outside.

"The fire's in the chimney, Sam," said Trevor. "Look!"

"We'll fight it from above," said Sam. He stood on Jupiter's platform. **"Extend, Elvis!"**

Sam was lifted into the air. When he was over the chimney he shouted, **"Water on, Elvis!"**

A few minutes later, the fire was out.

Afterwards, Bella made more pizzas. Four of them.

There was one for Sam. "Ee's-a my 'ero!" said Bella.

There was one for Dilys.

One for Mandy.

And one more for Norman.

"Mamma mia!" said Norman. "Yummy pizzas, Bella!"

Station Officer Steele wanted to find a mascot for the fire station. Would it be Woolly, Dusty or Rosa? Find out in . . .

Bath Time for Dusty

Sarah and James were playing with Dusty outside Dilys' shop. James read a notice in the window. "Station Officer Steele wants a mascot for the fire station," he said. "Dusty could do that! He'd be a great mascot!"

The twins took Dusty to the fire station.

"He's perfect, Uncle Sam," said Sarah.

Norman arrived with Woolly. "No, here's your mascot, Sam!" he said.

"Baaaaa!" said Woolly. He ran off. They found him eating the fire station flowers!

"Get rid of that thing!" said Station Officer Steele. "I'm looking for Rosa. Have you seen her?"

Steele put his hand on the flower tub. He didn't see Rosa sleeping there.

Rosa got a fright. **"Meeow!"** She scratched his hand!

"Yeeow!" cried Steele. "That cat is not going to be the mascot!"

Sam winked. "Dusty's got a good chance now," he said. "Once he's had a bath!"

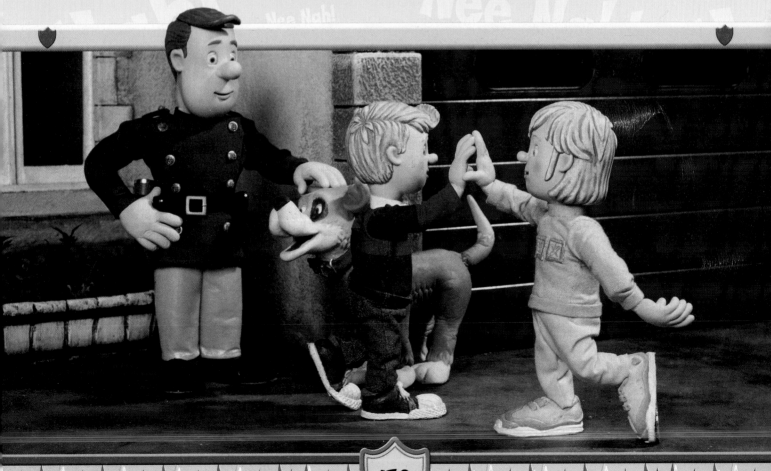

James filled a big tin bath with water. Dusty didn't like the look of it.

"Jump in, Dusty," said James. "It's only water . . ."

ONLY WATER! thought Dusty. **ONLY WATER?**

James held out a dog biscuit to get Dusty into the bath.

Dusty grabbed it – but James ended up in the water instead!

James and Sarah went to find Dusty. They saw him when he popped out of a dustbin!

Dusty ran to the Mountain Rescue Station to hide.

Mike Flood was working there. But when he turned on his blowtorch, it started a fire!

Sam and the crew went to put out the fire.

Dusty thought it was safe to come out. But the hoses were still on and he got soaked. Dusty got a bath, after all!

Now that he was clean, Steele said Dusty could be the station mascot.

Sarah took a photograph of him in his special outfit.

"Smile please, Uncle Sam!" said Sarah. "Smile, please, Dusty!"

"**Woof!**" said Dusty.

First prize in the Fun Run was one of Bella's cakes. Norman really wanted to win it. Find out if he did in . . .

Fun Run

Norman wanted to win the Fun Run race. The first prize was one of Bella's yummy cakes!

Sam and Tom put out markers. They started and ended at the fire station. They fixed red arrows to trees and fences. They were to show the runners where to go.

On the day of the race, the runners stood in a line. "Take your marks!" said Sam.

Naughty Norman tied Sarah
and James' laces together!

"Follow the red arrows,"
said Sam. "Ready? Get set, **GO!**"

Sarah and James tripped!

By the time Sam untied them,
the others were a long

way ahead.

Norman and Mandy were in the lead. Then Norman fired a water pistol at Mandy! She stopped, and he raced away.

Norman saw a red arrow. He smiled a sneaky smile. Then he turned the arrow round! **"Hee, hee!"** he said. "The others will go the wrong way now!"

He did the same thing with another arrow.

But Woolly was chewing the next arrow! "Oh, no," said Norman. "Now I don't know which way to go!"

Sarah, James and Mandy followed the arrows. They climbed stiles and ran through muddy puddles.

Back at the station, Sam was worried. "They should be back by now," he said.

"We'll send out a search party," said Steele.

Norman found an old shed. He stopped for a rest.

Mandy and Sarah arrived. They were carrying James! "An arrow pointed up a tree," he said. "I climbed it and fell."

"Er, who turned the arrows round?" asked Norman.

"We didn't say anything about turning arrows round!" said Mandy. "Norman, you're a cheat!"

They heard the **whirr!** of Tom's helicopter. But he didn't see them. He flew away.

Mandy had an idea. She put lots of bits of wood and twigs on the ground. They made an arrow shape!

Tom saw it and Sam sped to the rescue!

Steele gave out the Fun Run prizes. Mandy, Sarah and James got Bella's cake to share.

There was one of Elvis' rock cakes for Norman.

"Yuck!" said Norman.

At Christmas, we
always have a big tree in
Pontypandy. But one year
there were no trees
left. Read about
what happened
to Norman when
he tried to get
one in . . .

Let It Snow

It was Christmas in Pontypandy. But the garden centre had sold out of Christmas trees!

"There are trees on Pontypandy Mountain," Norman told Mandy. "We'll get one of them. Dusty can pull the sledge."

But Dusty couldn't pull both of them. So Norman went on his own.

On the mountain, Dusty ran under a low branch. The snow gave Norman a white beard! "Yo, ho, ho!" he said. "I'm Santa!"

Norman stopped near a cave. He tried to pull up a tree.

Snow slid down the mountain. It knocked Norman into the cave!

"Help!" cried Norman. He was stuck!

Dusty ran back to Pontypandy. Mandy told Dilys where Norman had gone.

"He'll freeze without a vest!" said Dilys. She phoned Fireman Sam.

"**Action stations!**" said Station Officer Steele.

The alarm bell rang. Sam and Elvis jumped into Jupiter. Her blue lights flashed and her siren wailed, **Nee Nah! Nee Nah!** Sam drove off. He took Dusty with them.

"Show us where Norman is, Dusty!" said Sam, when they reached the mountain.

Dusty ran to the cave. **"Woof, woof!"** he said.

"Start digging!" Sam told Elvis and Penny.

They dug into the snow.

"Is that you, Sam?" Norman shouted. "Hurry up, I've got a numb bum!"

Sam got Norman out of the cave. He took him home. "You mustn't go off on your own again," he said.

"But I wanted to get a Christmas tree," said Norman.

Just then, Tom's helicopter arrived. He dropped fairy lights on to a tall tree.

"Hey! A Christmas tree!" smiled Norman.

That night, everyone went to see the Christmas tree.

Norman gave Dusty a big bone, tied up with a ribbon. "Thanks for finding me, Dusty," he said. "Three cheers for Dusty! Hip, hip, hurray!"

"Woof!" said Dusty.

Bob the Builder

Bobsville is a busy town where there's always lots of building and work to do.

Bob the Builder runs a building yard. He can build and mend all sorts of things!

Wendy is Bob's partner. She's a great builder, too!

Pilchard is Bob's cat. She likes eating, sleeping and chasing mice!

Scoop the digger is the leader of Bob's machine team.

Dizzy is a little orange cement mixer.

Lofty is a mobile crane.

Roley the steamroller loves singing with his friend, **Bird**.

Muck the digger-dumper just loves being mucky!

There's a building supplies yard in Bobsville.

JJ owns the yard. Bob gets the things he needs there. **Trix** is JJ's forklift truck.

Molly is JJ's daughter. She hires out skips.

There's a farm near Bobsville, too.

Farmer Pickles is a farmer. **Scruffty** is his happy-yappy puppy.

Travis is the farm tractor.

Spud the scarecrow's job is to scare crows.

We put up a fence to stop the rabbits eating Farmer Pickles' cabbages. But something – or someone – knocked it down. Find out who it was in . . .

Bob and the Badgers

Rabbits had started eating Farmer Pickles' cabbages!

Bob and the team made a fence to keep them out.

"The rabbits won't get in now," said Bob.

"Spud's going to stay here tonight," said Farmer Pickles.

"Just in case."

"Yeah," said Spud. "Scare-rabbit Spud's on the job!"

That night, the rabbits came back but they couldn't get over the fence.

Spud was tired. He lay down and fell asleep . . . **Zzzzzzz!**

Two big badgers came along and knocked down the fence.

Sleepy Spud didn't see them!

In the morning, Farmer Pickles saw the broken fence.

"Look at those big paw prints!" said Spud. "A monster must have made them!"

"I'll follow the prints to find out what made them," said Farmer Pickles. "Wait here."

"What if the m-m-monster comes?" said Spud.

"There are no such things as monsters, Spud," Farmer Pickles replied.

Wendy went with Farmer Pickles. They found lots of black and white hairs.

"Badgers!" said Farmer Pickles. "They always use the same paths. The fence was in their way. So they knocked it down!"

"We need to let the badgers in and keep the rabbits out," said Wendy. "I'll ask Bob to help."

Bob was at his house. He had just finished fitting a cat flap in the door for Pilchard. It gave him an idea!

Bob went to the farm. He made a flap in the wire fence.

"There," he said. "A badger flap! The big badgers can open it, but the little rabbits can't!"

"Ruff!" said Scruffty. He tried the flap. It worked!

That night, Bob and the team went back to the farm. They hid, and watched the cabbage patch.

Along came the badgers. They pushed the badger flap open and walked through.

"Clever badgers!" said Muck.

"Clever Bob!" said Wendy.

When we were
working at the farm,
things kept going missing.
Find out who had taken
them in . . .

Scruffty On Guard

Farmer Pickles got some pigs.

"I need some sties for them to live in," he said. "I'll ring Bob."

Bob and the team set off for the farm.

"Can we build it?" said Scoop.

"Yes we can!" said the others.

"Er . . . yeah . . . I think so," said Lofty.

The pigs were in the barn. Humpty, the daddy pig, was in one pen. The mummy pig and her babies were in the other. Bob was busy building the sties when Farmer Pickles arrived.

"Have you seen my cap, Bob?" he said. "I can't find it."

Bob shook his head. He looked around. "That's funny," he said. "My lunch box is missing, too."

Soon after, Farmer Pickles' gloves disappeared.

"I'll leave Scruffty here tonight," said Farmer Pickles. "He'll guard the tools."

That night, Spud arrived to keep Scruffty company.

"Let's play fetch," said Spud. He threw a long stick and they both ran after it.

Now no one was guarding the tools!

Next morning, Bob's hammer was missing.

"Did you see anything, Scruffty?" asked Farmer Pickles.

Scruffty hung his head and walked away.

"I wonder if Scruffty has anything to do with this?" said Farmer Pickles.

The next thing to go missing was Bob's phone!

"I'll call the number on my phone," said Wendy. "The rings will lead us to it."

Ring, ring! Bob's phone was in the barn! **Ring, ring!** It was in Humpty's pen! So were all the other things.

"Ruff!" said Scruffty. He dug at the straw and uncovered a big hole. That was how Humpty had got out!

Soon, the sties were ready and Humpty and his family moved in.

"Oink! Oink!" they said. **"Oink! Oink!"**

"I think they like them!" said Bob.

Farmer Pickles gave Scruffty a big dog biscuit. "It's to say well done for finding the hole," he said.

"Ruff!" said Scruffty.

I made a tent for Dizzy and Muck when they camped out at the farm. But someone else ended up sleeping in it. Find out who in . . .

Dizzy and Muck Go Camping

Bob and the team went to Farmer Pickles' farm. They were going to build a campsite!

"Er, what **is** a campsite?" asked Dizzy.

"It's a place where people go for a holiday," said Bob. "They put up tents to sleep in. They cook food on a campfire and sing songs."

"Brilliant!" said Dizzy.

The first job was to build the shower block.

But the field was full of sheep. Bob had to put them into a pen. It took a long time.

"I'll come back tomorrow," he told Farmer Pickles.

Dizzy asked Bob if she could camp out with Muck.

"OK," said Bob. He made a frame and put a cover over it.

"Our very own tent!" said Dizzy. "Great!"

When it got dark, Spud arrived. He sat down near Dizzy's pretend camp fire.

"I like pretend games," said Spud. "I'm pretending to cook sausages on the fire."

"And we can sing a **real** campfire song," said Dizzy.

After a few songs, Spud was tired. He went back through the sheep pen to the barn.

"BAA! BAA!" Loud sheep noises woke Dizzy and Muck in the morning.

There were sheep everywhere!

"Oh, no," said Dizzy. "We forgot to close the gate!"

Dizzy and Muck pretended to be sheep dogs. **"Ruff! Ruff!"** they said. **"Ruff-ruff-ruff!"**

"Baaaaa!" The sheep ran back into the pen.

Bob and the team arrived to build the showers.

Bob made a floor. Then he built the walls and put on the roof. It was hard work!

He sat down in Dizzy and Muck's tent. It was warm and cosy. "I'll just have a little rest," he said.

"Zzzzzzzzz!" Bob fell asleep!

Farmer Pickles arrived. "Are you camping out as well, Bob?" he asked.

Bob woke up. "Oh, I was . . . er . . . just waiting for you," said Bob.

Dizzy whizzed around. "Camping's good fun, isn't it, Bob?" she asked.

Bob stretched. **"Yes, it is!"** he said.

Spud the scarecrow likes being helpful. Read all about how he made a special house for his new friends in . . .

Spud and the Doves

Mr Dixon took two white doves to Mr Ellis. He was going to use them in his magic tricks.

Spud arrived with some eggs for Mr Ellis. "Nice birdies!" said Spud.

"Coo, coo!" said the doves.

"Bob's making a house for them," Mr Ellis told Spud. "It's called a dovecote. It'll be ready when I get back from work."

"Can I look after the doves for you?" asked Spud.

"Yes," said Mr Ellis. "But don't let them out of the cage."

Spud liked the doves. They were good fun.

He stood on one leg and said, **"Coo, coo!"**

The doves copied him! **"Coo, coo!"**

Spud found Mr Ellis' magic cloak. He put it over the cage.

"Abracadabra!" he said. "Magic Spud will make the

doves disappear."

He pulled off the cloak. But the doves were still there!

Spud opened the cage door and looked inside.

"Abracadabra!" he said. The doves flew out!

They flew around and landed on the thatch roof.

"Oh, no!" said Spud. "Here, dovey-doveys! You were supposed to go invisible, not fly away."

Spud climbed up on to the roof. But his foot went through the straw. "Help!" he called. **"I'm stuck!"**

Soon, Bob and Lofty arrived.

"Why are you up on the roof?" asked Bob.

"I was trying to catch the doves," said Spud. "My foot went through the roof. Now I'm stuck!"

Not for long! Lofty lifted him down.

Spud got the doves back inside the cage.

Then Bob's friend Katie came to fix the hole in Mr Ellis' roof.

Bob showed Spud the dovecote. But Spud grabbed it, and pulled off the roof! "Oh, no!" said Spud.

So Katie made a new straw roof for the dovecote and Spud made a little bird for the top.

"Coo, coo, coo!" said the doves. They liked the dovecote. So did Spud. He flapped his arms like wings. "Coo, coo!" he said. "I'm Spud the dove!"

Humphrey the pig made a real mess of the Winter Fair. But we all worked together to fix it up again. Read how we did it in . . .

Mr Bentley's Winter Fair

Bob and the team were all helping Mr Bentley with the Winter Fair.

Mr Bentley pointed to a map. It showed them where the stalls had to go.

Bob and Wendy's first job was to put up the Christmas lights. Then they had to blow up the big Santa and fix him to the Town Hall.

Farmer Pickles and Travis arrived with Humphrey the pig. He was for the **Guess the Weight of the Pig** contest.

"The gate on Humphrey's pen is not safe," said Mr Bentley. "I'll get Bob to fix it."

Spud sat by the pig pen to eat his pizza. **"Oink!"** said Humphrey. He pushed open the gate and ran off with the pizza!

Wendy filled the blow-up Santa with air. He bobbed and bounced around. "Hold on to the rope, Wendy!" said Bob.

Mr Bentley tried to help. He held a rope, but Santa bobbed around and kicked him!

Humphrey ran by with Spud chasing. "Stop that pig!" he yelled.

Humphrey bumped into Mr Bentley. The aerial on his talkie-talkie made a hole in Santa. **PSSSSSST!** The air escaped. Santa went all floppy!

"**Oink! Oink!**" said Humphrey. He bumped into Mrs Potts' stall, then he knocked Mrs Percival's stall over too. Everything fell off!

"**Oink! Oink!**" said Humphrey. He bashed into JJ's stall next.

But then Humphrey stopped. "**Oink!**" He smelled pizza! He ran to Mr Sabatini's stall. He knocked the pizzas off the table and ate them!

"What a mess!" said Mr Bentley. "The Winter Fair is ruined. Just ruined."

"Don't worry, Mr Bentley," said Bob. "If we all work together we can fix it."

Bob was right. Everyone helped.

Spud got Humphrey back into his pen.

"Well done, Spud!" said Mr Bentley.

And Wendy fixed Mrs Potts' and JJ's stalls.

Bob fixed Mrs Percival's stall. Then Wendy put a patch on Santa and blew him up again.

Mr Bentley ticked the jobs on his list. "All done!" he said.

Just then he got a call on his talkie-talkie. "Oh, no!" he said. "That was the Mayor. She wants me to do another Winter Fair next year!"

I love Christmas! It's a really special time of the year – especially when it snows! Read the story of how Farmer Pickles gave us a very special Christmas gift in . . .

The Christmas Tree

A few days before Christmas, Farmer Pickles asked Bob to come to the farm. "You can cut down one of my Christmas trees," he told Bob. "It will really brighten up the yard."

The whole team went to the farm.

"Where's the tree?" asked Bob.

"I'll show you!" said Spud. "It's the big one on the edge of my field! Over there!"

Scoop used his snowplough to clear snow away from the tree.

Then Muck moved the soil away from it.

Lofty tried to pull the tree out of the ground. But it was big and heavy. **"Oo-er!"** he said. "Very heavy, very heavy!"

With an extra-big pull, Lofty got the tree out.

Lofty put the tree into Muck's dumper.

Then Muck took it back to the yard.

"Put the tree into this big red bucket, Lofty," said Wendy.

"It looks great!" said Bob. "Now we can decorate it."

Bob put the fairy lights on the tree.

Wendy added shiny tinsel and coloured baubles.

Lofty brought presents and put them under the tree.

"Now for the best bit," said Bob. "It's time to turn on the lights!"

Everyone cheered when the tree was lit up.

All except Wendy.

"What's wrong?" asked Bob.

"I don't know," said Wendy. "There's something missing. But I don't know what it is."

Bird arrived. He sat right at the top of the tree. **"Toot!"** he whistled. **"Toot, toot!"**

"That's it!" said Wendy. "We need something for the top of the Christmas tree. But not Bird!"

Bird flew down to the decorations box. He picked one up in his beak. Then he flew up to the top of the Christmas tree with it.

Can you guess what Bird put on top of the Christmas tree?

Yes, it was a shiny, silver star!

"Toot!" said Bird.

"Clever Bird!" said Wendy.

The team all cheered. "Hurray!"

"Perfect!" said Bob. "And look – it's snowing again!

Merry Christmas, everyone!"

The End